1.95/11.88

maus. 11/89

ACL

D0842110

ACL

DANNY'S CHRISTMAS STAR

Edith Kunhardt

Greenwillow Books, New York

Magic Markers and a black
pen were used for the
full-color art. The text
type is Avant Garde Gothic Book.

Copyright © 1989 by Edith Kunhardt
All rights reserved. No part of this book
may be reproduced or utilized in any form
or by any means, electronic or mechanical,
including photocopying, recording or by
any information storage and retrieval
system, without permission in writing
from the Publisher, Greenwillow Books,
a division of William Morrow & Company, Inc.,
105 Madison Avenue, New York, N.Y. 10016.
Printed in Hong Kong by South China Printing Co.
First Edition   10 9 8 7 6 5 4 3 2 1

Library of Congress
Cataloging-in-Publication Data

Kunhardt, Edith.
Danny's Christmas star
by Edith Kunhardt.
p.   cm.
Summary: After Danny
accidentally drops the
star for the Christmas tree,
he makes a replacement.
ISBN 0-688-07905-9.
ISBN 0-688-07906-7 (lib. bdg.)
[1. Christmas—Fiction.]
I. Title.   PZ7.K94905Dap 1989
[E]—dc19
88-18785   CIP   AC

To Martha and Neddy
and our Christmases

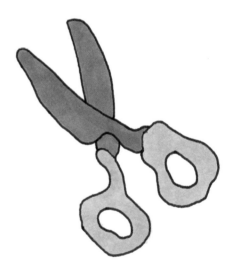

It is Christmas Eve.
Danny and his mother and father
are decorating the Christmas tree.

"It looks beautiful!" says Danny.
"Now you may put the star on top,"
says his father. "Climb up on my
shoulders."
Danny lifts the star from its box.
Suddenly it falls and breaks.

"Oh, no!" says Danny. "The star
is broken! Now what can we do?"
He begins to cry.
"Don't worry, Danny," says his
mother. "We'll get another star."

"But it's too late to buy one," says
Danny's father. "All the stores are
closed."
"Why don't you make a star, Danny?"
says his mother. "I'll give you some
scissors, some cardboard, and some
silver paper."

"All right," says Danny. He sits down
at the kitchen table to make the star.

Danny cuts the cardboard with the scissors.

He wraps silver paper around it.

Then he cuts out a hole for the hanger.

"Here's my star!" he cries, running
into the living room.

"It's perfect, Danny!" says Danny's
father. "Now get up on my shoulders."
Danny hangs the star on
the very top branch.

Later that night, Danny leaves
cookies and milk for Santa Claus.
"Santa always likes refreshments,"
says his father.

Danny hangs up his stocking.
"Santa may want to write us a note," says Danny's mother.
She puts out a pad and pencil.

Danny goes to bed.
"Good night, Danny," says his father,
kissing him. "Merry Christmas."
"Good night, Danny," says his mother,
tucking him in. "Remember, the sooner
you go to sleep, the sooner you'll
wake up."

In the morning, Danny and his mother and father open their stockings.

They line up to march into the living room. Danny is the youngest, so he goes first.

Danny runs to the tree. He opens
his presents. His very favorite one
is a new sled.
"I can't wait to go sledding!"
he cries.

Then Danny sees that Santa's milk
and cookies are all gone.
But there is a note.

Danny reads the note. It says,
"Dear Danny, Thank you for the
milk and cookies. I like your
new star. See you next year.

Love, Santa "

Danny looks up at the top of the tree.

"Merry Christmas, Star," he says.

The star sparkles back at him.

"Merry Christmas," it seems
to say.